Forever FRIENDS

KIARAH MICHELLE

JayMedia
Publishing

Printed in the United States of America

ISBN: 978-1-957443-04-1

First Printing, 2022

JayMedia Publishing

Laurel, MD 20708

www.publishing.jaymediagroup.net

CHAPTER 1

Beep, Beep, Beep. It was five a.m. on Monday morning, Ashley jumped out of bed, stretched her arms as she headed to her closet to get ready for the busy day ahead. She reached for her favorite pair of black leggings, put on a white short-sleeve shirt with a red sweater and a pair of red converses. Every morning is started with a sweet strawberry smoothie that she makes for her mom and herself to help boost energy for the day. First, on the schedule, was school from 7:30 am until 2 pm and after that was cheer practice. The biggest smile came upon her face walking into the gym to get practice started since she was the captain of the team. You wouldn't imagine someone smiling walking into the gym, because in the afternoon it smelled like sweat from all the gym classes that took place in there. All the new incoming freshmen cheerleaders would say, "Ashley rules like a dictator." It was her way or the highway. For example, every minute someone is late to practice, they have to run that number of laps around the track outside. Ashley didn't care if it was raining or muddy either, she would make you run outside. It was August with a temperature of 79 degrees, so all they had to worry about was not dying of heat exhaustion when running laps.

After being a tough cheer captain in the afternoon, it was off to church for dance practice at 5:30 in the evening. After walking into the sanctuary and changing into her jazz shoes, she saw her best friend Asia, who was more like a sister to her. They commence to perform the handshake that they do every time they see each other and then began to stretch at the front of the room. At this practice, she would be learning a new dance and would be placed in the front center position. The position was directly in front of the podium where the pastor preaches on Sundays. You knew it was the center because there was a line going straight down the center aisle that was visible in the green stain-filled carpet. It was well-known that the other dancers had a friend that only discussed bad things about Ashley with them. These dancers were a little jealous because they believed she was only able to be in front as a result of her aunt being the choreographer. A new dance was taught by Jordan, the other head choreographer, and not by Ashley's aunt.

The time was 8:30 pm, the sun had gone down, streetlights were on, and the church parking lot was empty. Ashley was always the last to leave due to waiting for her mom to stop conversing with her friends. Not to mention that homework still had to be done and she had dinner to eat before she could rest. This busy lifestyle was not normal for a 16-year-old girl but it was balanced by having great friends around her who wouldn't take anything away from her such as her center position at dance or captain title at cheer. Or so Ashley thought.

The next Monday came around and at 5:30 pm, she walked into the church sanctuary and placed her bookbag down on the green floor. Sitting on the floor and beginning to pull her jazz shoes out of her bookbag to change, she heard a high-pitched voice. Before looking up. she kicked off her right cheer shoe and put on her jazz shoe. She heard the voice say, "I'm so nervous to start dancing here!" Hurriedly kicking off her other cheer shoe to put the other jazz shoe on, she looked up and saw a new light-skinned girl stretching on the floor with the rest of her friends. Ashley slowly stood up, turned toward the doors and speed-walked to the bathroom. As Ashley walked into the bathroom, three of the younger dancers walked out discussing the sleepover that they had over the weekend. Appearing to be alone, she looked at herself in the mirror and said, "I'm fine. I've got nothing to worry about." While looking in the mirror, a young girl's voice said to Ashley, "You need to be the best dancer and an all-around perfect person." Ashley turned around quickly to see who it was. A loud toilet flush filled the room and a young girl who dances with Ashley, stepped out of the stall. "Oh, it's you!" The young girl proceeded to say, "The new girl will take everything from you." In response, Ashley said, "Look, I got this. No one will ever replace me!" While walking up to the sink to wash her hands and staring in the mirror, the girl said, "You won't like this new girl! Your life will change!"

Based on what her friend in the bathroom said, Ashley vowed to not let the new girl come and turn her world upside down. In the same dance practice, the girls were lined up in the front of the sanctuary in front of the pulpit. The new girl was standing directly next to Ashley. Jordan walked up and said, "Ladies, this is Lauren. She will be joining us and taking the center position." Frown lines immediately appeared upon Ashley's face as she slowly stepped to the side in her new position without saying a word. In her mind, that was strike one. After dance practice, Ashley sat in the lobby of the church watching everyone leave wanting to speak to her young friend again. Unfortunately, she did not see her so she must have left early.

CHAPTER 2

That was the beginning of what started Ashley's issue with Lauren and what eventually became the problem that started the separation between Ashley and her best friend Asia. Back at dance practice, Ashley stood in the lobby, pacing back and forth, deciding how to act when she walked in. Ashley stood on her tiptoes and looked in the window of the sanctuary doors. She saw Asia stretching and laughing with Lauren. She squinted her eyes because she didn't like what she was seeing. She stepped back and sat in one of the lobby chairs when the front doors opened and in walked the young girl that warned Ashley about the new girl. Ashley said, "I've been texting you." The girl responded, "I only have one thing to say to you today. End her before she ends you! Do not show your jealousy."

Walking into practice like normal, Ashley saw Asia, but no handshake was done. Only a simple, "Hi" and hug was given to her. Stunned, she stood in place for a minute, blinking her eyes three times to make sure that just happened. She was completely thrown off guard. As a result, she acted like she didn't care, walked over to her other dance friend Megan and tried to start a conversation about cheer. Stunning her again, Megan said, "Oh Ash, guess who joined my rec team... Lauren. Turns out she cheers too. Isn't that great!" Blinking her eyes three times and pinching herself to see if she was dreaming, all Ashley could say was,

"Seriously." She walked to the front of the room to begin practice but was again pushed to the side. There were sudden changes that Ashley didn't like such as how the choreographer Jordan began asking for suggestions from Lauren when she would normally ask Ashley for them.

Breathing heavily with her arms folded and eyes squinted, a wave of anger grew inside of her, and Ashley felt like a bully was emerging. She started making fun of how thick Lauren was and how she was so white she could blend in with a plain white wall. Although it was mean, it made Ashley feel a little bit better. The first impression of Lauren was that she was pretty, had long hair, and could sing. Lots of people thought Ashley could not sing and it was a known fact that she always wanted long hair which gave her plausible reason to be jealous of Lauren. The first reason was for not being in the front for several dances, then Asia not doing the handshake lately, Lauren now sitting next to Jordan during church where Ashley used to sit, and even Ashley's mom calling Lauren a goddaughter. Everyone was in love with Lauren and her personality. It was like everyone was under her spell including Asia.

It was Friday night and time for the *Bad Girls Club* watch party, where the dance group spent most of their time together discussing everything - the good and bad topics - while watching their favorite TV show. Asia put some chips and salsa on the dinner table for the adults and some in the living room for the other girls coming over in preparation for the Friday night hangout. After laying the chips and salsa out, Asia sat on the couch and kept turning her head back and forth to the clock on the wall anxiously awaiting Ashley's arrival. The first to arrive was dance member Megan and her mom that everyone called, "T", who Asia met through Ashley because they both grew up cheering in the recreational circuit. Second was Lauren and her mom Erica, who were excited to be invited to their first watch party. They walked in with goodie bags for all the moms and girls. Lauren and Megan became close friends from figuring out they live down the street from each other and began cheering on the same team. Everyone has had a chance to fall under Lauren's spell and build a friendship with her. While all the moms gather in the dining room with their glasses of wine, Asia's mom Renee could see that her daughter was still nervous. She could tell by the way Asia was shaking her leg while sitting and banging her fist together. As she walked out of the dining room, her mom said, "Asia, come into the kitchen please." She took a deep breath and went to the kitchen. Her mom asked, "What's up?" In response, Asia said, "I plan on talking to Ash about Lauren. I have to know why she is being a bully to her." Her mom walked to the fridge with no response. She took out the pitcher of lemonade, poured it in five glasses and placed them on a tray for Asia to give to Megan, Lauren, and Ashley. While her mom was doing that, Asia arched her eyebrows as if she was processing what was just said to her. Walking back to Asia with the tray, her mom said, "Daughter, remember there could always be a deeper issue." Asia walked back to the living room, sat the tray down, and all the girls present grabbed a cup. Still nervous, Asia grabbed her cup with a shaking hand and took a sip.

With five minutes until *Bad Girls Club* was to start, Ashley was still not here. After a minute, Ashley walked in with her mom Nicole. With a smile on her face, she greeted with a confident "Hey," because this was the place, she knew she wouldn't lose to Lauren. Everyone said "Hi" back to her and hugged her saying, "You made it just in time!" Plopping on the couch right in between Lauren and Asia, Ashley proceeded to do her handshake with Asia. An hour had passed, and all the moms were laughing loudly in the kitchen as they reminisced on past adventures. All the girls were laughing at the final scene of the premiere episode. As the credits roll, Megan went to the bathroom and Lauren slid to the floor to stretch out. When the episode ends, Asia asks Ashley, "Why don't you like Lauren?" Startled by the question, Ashley stared with a blank face and blinked three times. Lauren turned her head so fast to look at Ashley with a puppy dog sad face because she was curious about the answer too. Ashley's face had a look of terror because she did not want to admit that she was scared of losing everything to Lauren. Walking downstairs to the front door, Asia's mom called out, "Pizza's here girls," at the same time Megan walked out of the bathroom and notices the weird tension in the room. She sat back down in her chair and asked, "Why so silent?" With no response from Ashley, Asia turned to Megan and said, "I asked Ash why she doesn't like Lauren." In response, "Oh yeah, seriously Ash, what is the problem?" asked Megan. Ashely remained sitting with a blank face and giving no response. Realizing that Ashley was not going to give a response, Asia then proceeded to say, "Well, Lauren's birthday dinner is coming up and I know it's on a day we planned to hangout but I'm gonna go to her dinner instead." Ashley continued her blank stare.

It was 9:00 p.m. and almost time for the second episode of the two-part premiere of *Bad Girls Club* to air. With the question still lingering over her head and the declaration made by Asia, Ashley had no idea what to do. Megan stood up from sitting in her chair, grabbed her lemonade and walked over to the couch to sit next to Ashley. She said, "I'm going too. We are all her friends, and you should be too." Asia's mom had come back upstairs and placed two pizza boxes and napkins on the ottoman on her way back into the dining room. Coming in behind Asia's mom was the young girl Ashley met at the same dance practice when Lauren started. She even grabbed the fifth cup of lemonade that Ashley thought was just extra and walked into the kitchen. Not sure what to do next, Ashley grabbed a slice of pizza, a napkin and finished her drink in silence. The *Bad Girls Club* opening song began to play and the second episode started. The room was still silent, Asia's legs was nervously shaking, Megan was awkwardly staring into her phone, and Lauren was just sitting on the floor watching TV still curious to hear from Ashley. "I need more lemonade," Ashley said as she stood up to walk to the kitchen. Sitting at the table drinking her lemonade, the friend said, "You are losing everything dance, friends, what's next?" Ashley sat down at the table too and said to the friend, "This is strike two." Before leaving the kitchen, the girl said, "Don't show your weakness, find a change." Walking back into the living room and sitting down in her spot on the couch, Ashley joined in on the laughter at the scene taking place on TV. In the back of her head, she was thinking about what change needed to happen. The night ended in silence and with that question never getting answered.

CHAPTER 3

Knock, Knock. Asia's bedroom door opened and her mom said, "Asia, it's 6:30 a.m. let's get up and get ready for school." She stood in the doorway with one hand on her hip and the other on the doorknob with her head tilted to the side. Asia kicked her blanket to the floor and sat up in bed while staring at the wall for five minutes without moving. Seeing that she had finally gotten up, Asia's mom sighed heavily and walked downstairs to the kitchen to finish breakfast. Because Asia attends a private school, her mom takes her to school since there were no buses, one plus side was that she was able to wake up later than the other girls in the dance group. Another plus side to private school was not having to spend lots of time in the morning picking out an outfit because she wore the same thing every day. Asia got out of bed and went to her bathroom. She proceeded to brush her teeth, wash her face, and put her hair into a slick high ponytail. She went to her closet and grabbed her uniform which is a black knee length skirt and a white button up shirt. She wears whatever type of shoe she wants which is always black boots.

The time was 7:15 a.m. Walking into the kitchen, Asia smelled the fresh bacon and eggs that her mom just made. A bacon and egg sandwich is her favorite thing to eat in the morning. She took a big bite of her sandwich while looking at the calendar that hung on the fridge and began to choke on her food. She ran to the trash to spit her food out. Asia's mom said, "What is wrong with you?" In response, she walks over to the fridge points at the calendar and said, "It's the first Monday in September which means it's the first practice for anniversary." Confused as to why this made her daughter choke Asia's mom said, "Look, meet me downstairs in the car. It's time to go." Asia grabbed her bookbag, looked at the calendar again and walked to meet her mom in the car.

Why is the first Monday in September such a big deal? Asia knew that this meant it was the first practice for anniversary, and Asia knew how important this night was to Ashley. It is where she shines the most. While in the car on her way to school, Asia had a worried look on her face. Asia's worried look is when her eyebrows are arched down, and her head is resting on her right shoulder. In her mind, she was worried about the problems that could result in Lauren being able to dance for anniversary. Lifting her head up, she said, "Mom, I texted Ash and apologized for putting her on the spot in front of everyone on Friday, but she hasn't responded. It's been two days and today is the beginning of anniversary." Placing her arm over Asia's chest, because she just braked hard at a stop light, her mom responded, "Give her time. All you can do is be the best friend that you are to all of your friends but remember it could be something deeper."

The time was 2:30pm and Asia was in her eighth period class, but all day she has been worried about Lauren and Ashley. At lunch, her friends asked these questions, "Why are you silent?" "What's going on?" "Did you not sleep good?" All Asia did in response was nod her head and say, "I'm fine." And then she went back to being silent and staring off into space. Asia's eighth period class was where she learned about the bible. The teacher was going over how you must listen to those who came before you. Immediately, she thought about what her mother said about being the best friend that she could be. Asia asked herself, How can I be friends with Lauren and Ash? Will Ash be mad, If I dance with Lauren more this anniversary year? Is Ashley mad about not being in the center for one song? On the ride home, Asia said, "Mom, I'm gonna take your advice. I've tried reaching out to Asia but I'm still going to be the best friend that I can to Lauren." At home Asia sent Lauren a text asking her to come to practice early so they can discuss anniversary.

It was 4:30pm, an hour before dance started and Lauren and Ashley were at the front talking about what typically happens at anniversary. Jordan walked in and saw the two just talking at the front. She walked over to the sound booth, called out Asia's name and gestured for her to come to the booth. Jordan asked, "Are you and Ash, okay? I noticed you didn't handshake last week and you've been spending more time with Lauren rather than Ash." Not wanting everyone to be all up in her business Asia responded, "We are all good and walks away." Heading out to the bathroom, she looked at herself in the mirror, scrunched her eyes and eyebrows, tilted her head to side and thought to herself, Maybe it's me, I'm the reason she doesn't like Lauren because I haven't been treating her the same. I completely forgot about the handshake. Wondering what to do at today's practice when she sees Ashley, she put a smile on her face, walked into the sanctuary and began to teach Lauren some past opening dances before practice starts. In just thirty minutes Lauren learned an entire past opening anniversary dance and they made plans to go to the movies together. Walking to her book bag that was in the pew closest to the exit door, Asia thought to herself, Until Ash pulls through, I will be the best friend that I can to Lauren since she is new.

CHAPTER FOUR

"*Ash,* are you still with us?" Three out of four teachers asked Ashley since she seems not herself due to the actions of not answering questions when called on, running late to each class, and wearing sweatpants to school which she almost never did. In all classes, Ashley sat in the back with her head down on the table staring at the floor or she sat staring out the window completely zoning everyone out. It was 2:30pm -time for cheer practice- and guess who ran five laps for being five minutes late? It was Ashley! She even let her co-captain lead stretches and count out the routine while she barely uttered a word the entire practice. The time was 5:30pm and Ashley was in the car with her mom on the way to dance practice. She sat slouching in the seat with one leg propped up on the arm rest, wearing a hoodie covering the entirety of her face along with headphones blocking out the rest of the world noises. It was clear that Ashley was not in her best mood and that not speaking to Asia for two days had affected her. There was a text message that read, "I am sorry for putting you on the spot like that in front of everyone. I should have asked when it was just us." But Ashley didn't respond because she felt if they were truly best friends, it should not have happened in the first place.

This was THEE practice for Ashley. It set the tone for anniversary. It was known that whoever danced on the higher platform stage was the best in the ministry. There was always rivalry between the teenage girls because they were always watching to see who danced the leads, performed in the most songs, and received the most solos. For the past couple of years, Ashley had been one of the best in the dance ministry. This rehearsal was important because it was opening song day, it was the beginning of the anniversary performance, all the groups in the dance ministry danced together and it was choreographed by the other choreographer Jordan who had been accused of showing favorites before too.

After stretching, everyone was standing around waiting on their placements. Lauren and Asia were waiting in the right corner by the drums, the baby girls were waiting in the center, the older adults were sitting on the floor, and Ashley was waiting in the far-left corner by the big piano. Jordan came up, took Asia to the high stage and placed her in the center. Ashley's one friend came up behind her and said, "That's okay as long as you're up there on the high stage too, right? Isn't that all that matters – either being on the high stage or in the center?" Jordan then called out for Lauren, placed her to the left of Asia and said that it will be the three of them on the high stage and everyone else on the floor. Asia made a sharp head turn to look at Ashley and made a sad face at her. Looking up at Jordan and then Asia, Ashley's stomach dropped but that wasn't strike three yet. Ashley sat down on the floor and listened to her friend some more who said, "Man, imagine what you could do up there. Is that fair? You've been here longer than the both of them and have known Jordan longer." Out loud Ashley said, "Yeah, I know right." Everyone looked and stared at Ashley because of how loud she was. The friend then said, "As long as you're dancing in the lower front, right? Isn't being in front all that really matters?" Jordan came off the high stage to place the rest of the group on the floor. She began placing the four baby girls in a line going up the center aisle and Ashley's aunt in the center. The four adults are in a straight line on the floor while the rest of teenage girls are in a line behind them. To everyone's surprise, Ashley was at the very end of the teenage line and was in the corner by the drums with little to no room to really move. The "best" part of this entire practice - the part that really started Ashley's rage - was that she only got to dance for the last minute of a 6-minute song. Now, that was strike three!

On the ride home, Ashley was still in shock about what should've been her favorite practice but instead was a nightmare. During the car ride, a decision was made that ultimately decided the fate of Ashley and Asia's friendship. She pulled out her phone and blocked Asia on all social media and blocked her number. Arriving at her house and slamming her mom's car door, Ashley stomped heavily up the steps, slammed her bedroom door, and threw her bookbag down on the chair because her nerves had been struck. Hiding in her closet, sitting on top of the pile of clothes that she chose not to wear this morning, crying, Ashley wrote in her journal about her feelings and how her life was falling apart. Losing her best friend and losing her spot in the opening dance for her favorite time of year was not at all where Ashley saw this year going. Continuing to reflect on what had happened, Ashley remembered that her friend said, "A change needs to happen." She felt that the two people who started dancing after her took everything she loved. Lying down, facing the closet ceiling, staring into the eyes of a Chris Brown Poster that she put there years ago, she asked herself, Should I be happy dancing in a corner? Will people still watch me and love my dancing the same? Sitting up and putting these two questions into her journal, Ashley wrote, "I wonder if I'll be happier just focusing on cheer. I am still the leader of that after all."

It was Tuesday morning at 6:30am. Every morning Ashley made a smoothie for her mom and tea for herself while they talked about the day ahead before heading out. Shaky and unsteady hands cause the milk for the smoothie to spill over the cup as Ashley poured it. Ashley's mom, Nicole, immediately rushed over and asked, "Are you okay?" She said it in a quick manner since she was afraid of the response. Ashley said, "I want to quit dancing at the church. Have a great day. Love you bye." She sped walked out of the front door to catch the bus to school. This was odd behavior for Ashley since she would normally let her mom drive her to school but she didn't want to hear her mom rant about why she shouldn't quit.

CHAPTER FIVE

Two weeks had gone by since Ashley's mom let her quit dance and it has also been two weeks of no contact with Asia. One Sunday came where it was Ashley's dance group's turn to perform at both services. However, Ashley was not dancing with them, but still had to be at service because of her mother's beliefs of being at church every Sunday. It was a painful three minutes. As her group got in their positions, the music started and she heard, "You're listening to the sound." She immediately made duck lips and squinted her eyes. That lyric was the beginning to her favorite song, the one that she had been wanting to dance to forever. Her face was blank and tears piled up in her eyes. She clenched her teeth to try to look as if she was okay with not dancing. When the dance ended, she walked out to the bathroom to cry in the stall, so no one could see that she was upset. After service, everyone loved to hang out in the sanctuary where they would hug, talk, and catch up with everyone. Someone who had been watching Ashley since she was two years old came up to her and said, "I was looking for you during the dance. Are you okay?" Shocked that someone noticed she was missing, "I'm okay just taking a break," Ashley replied. On the car ride home, instead of blasting music and singing the church hymns like normal, Ashley's mom kept the music off. They sat in silence for a while until her mom says, "Ash, I know you don't want to hear this, but I've always told you if it's for God then it does not matter where you are in the dance. People will see and feel you!"

A few more weeks went by and during her newfound free time, Ashley contributed even more to her cheer team, after all she is the captain. Instead of only having practices on weekdays the team started practicing on early Saturday mornings too.

A month had gone by. Ashley hadn't been to Asia's house for a girl's night in a month and a half and didn't want to be there. Many Friday nights went by where she sat in her room and watched *Bad Girls Club* by herself. There were many times where something funny happened and Ashley wanted to pick up the phone and call Asia. For instance, there was a scene where two girls poured glitter all into the beds of the girls they hate. That moment all Ash wanted to do was reminisce about that scene with her best friend because no one else, not even anyone on the cheer team, understood the comedy in *Bad Girls Club*. It was Friday night and a new season of BGC was about to air. Ashley was in her cheetah print onesie with a bag of unsalted pretzels and a glass of lemonade comfortably sitting in her bed waiting for the premiere to start, out of the blue, "ASH! Get dressed and let's go NOW!" her mom yelled. Startled, she knocked the bag of pretzels off her bed. She jumped out of bed, put on her cheer warm-up pants and jacket, slid her feet into her black crocs and rushed down the steps to meet her mom in the car. Ashley questioned, "Where are we going? The new Season of BGC is about to come on!" She got no response from her mother. It was a quiet ride, but once they got off the highway at the Dundalk exit it became noticeable that they were headed towards Asia's house. There was no other reason for Ash's mom to be driving in that direction. Meanwhile at Asia's house, Asia was sitting on the couch waiting for the premiere to start as well. The one friend from the dance group was there as well and was telling Asia how to act if she were to see Ash. After arriving, Ashley slugged her way up the steps. When the door opened and she saw Asia on the couch, she waved. Blowing her breath as she stood up, Asia took the remote, turned the TV off and walked into her bedroom, right past Ashley as if she is invisible. Asia slammed her door, turned on the TV in her bedroom and lied down on her bed. The premiere started but she couldn't even focus on it, because she didn't like how she had just treated Ashley - as if they weren't like sisters. She grabbed the remote, turned the TV off. She sat the remote on her nightstand and pulled on her lamp string so that she could sit in the dark. Watching the glow-in-the-dark green stars on her walls begin to light up, she went to sleep in sadness. Ashley sat on the couch next to her friend. "Are these the changes that had to be made - me losing my best friend and my spot on the dance team?" asked Ashley. Sitting back rolling her eyes, the friend said, "No, the change still needs to be made. It's not an environmental change. Think about what your mom said." A few more weeks went by.

Each Sunday a new dance was performed with Asia as the lead dancer while Ashley was competing in a cheer competition. They both went about their lives as if they didn't miss each other and didn't need to work on anything. Well, one Sunday came and Ashley's dance group was ministering to another favorite song of Ashley's and one minute into the song Ashley's head was buried deep between her knees, hiding her sadness of not dancing. Tired of not being able to enjoy church anymore back at home, Ashley took her journal and sat in her closet. She wrote down the words "I really miss dance" and "maybe I should go back," staring up at her Chris Brown poster, Ashley remembered that her friend said to make a change. To try something different and have something change Ashley decided to return to dance with a different mindset. It was 6pm, Asia and Lauren were stretching together in the center aisle, the baby dancers were lined up across the front, the choreographer was standing in the audio room and in walked Ashley back from her "break" from dance. She immediately walked over to the choreographer to let her know that she was back and went to stretch alone in the corner. A new dance was being learned. It was no surprise to Ashley but her placement was yet again stuck in a corner, but instead of getting mad she stuck it out and danced through it. Even through the performance on that Sunday, her all was given as if she was in the center, even from the corner. After the service, that same person from before came up to her and said, "Watching you dance for the Lord always makes me smile and brightens my day." This comment rattled Ashley, it made her realize that someone actually paid attention to her even when she wasn't in the center. She told her mom on the way home, and her mom replied, "See, I told you. It's not about where you are, it's how you dance, people will watch you." A new attitude had come upon Ashley. She was not going to complain about where she was placed and still danced to the fullest, not worrying about any new people. Although, there was still something missing from her life. She felt lonely and felt like she couldn't share her newfound experiences with her best friend because she had blocked her.

CHAPTER 6

It was the third Sunday in October and for some reason, Asia's mom didn't start buying new fall/Halloween decorations until this specific day. While her mom was out of the house all day, Asia was home dusting off the countertops that she knew pumpkins were going to be put on. After that, she lied down on her bed and turned on her TV to watch the Hocus Pocus movie marathon that only comes on this time of year. In between commercials, she scrolled through Instagram and she saw that a woman made a post about a live episode of *Bad Girls Club* and how they will show never seen before footage on Saturday at 6:00 p.m. Jumping up from her bed and racing down the steps to meet her mother at the front door, who just got back from getting groceries and decorations, Asia said, "Mom, we have to move girl's night to Saturday for this special live episode." Taking a big inhale and exhale and slamming her hand on the wall, her mom said, "Daughter, can you at least grab a bag of groceries and then bombard me." The next five minutes consisted of Asia running up and down the steps to help her mother take the groceries to the kitchen, putting them away and taking the decorations to the craft room which was next to her bedroom. As soon as she finished, she sat down at the kitchen table and called Lauren and Megan to invite them over Saturday for girls' night to watch this special episode. Asia picked up the pencil on the table and began tapping it on the table at a fast pace. Her leg was shaking super-fast as she picked up the phone to call Ashley. She called twice, there was no answer. Standing up to check the groceries to make sure they had everything, she noticed there was no lemonade. Walking into the kitchen to begin making dinner, Asia's mom saw her daughter looking through all of the cabinets and the refrigerator. She stood behind the sink with arms folded and head tilted to the side and observed her daughter acting frantic and concerned about what was happening Asia's mom said, "If you're looking for lemonade, there is none. The only person who drinks it is Ash. Since you've been avoiding her and it doesn't seem like she's coming on Saturday, I didn't get any lemonade." Slamming the cabinet door and walking back to her room Asia dove face first into her bed and screamed because she was angry with herself. She turned to lay on her back and stared to the left side of her room where on the wall is a picture of Ash and herself at the amusement park in matching clothes. She turned back over in frustration because she tried to reach out to Ashley, but nothing was working.

Ding Dong. Asia's mom headed downstairs to let Nicole in. The two moms decided to work together in an effort to get their daughters' friendship back together. The two moms had done their best to guide their daughters in the right direction without stepping in too much. Only they know how many fights and arguments they had survived to be the sistah-girls that they are now. "Did you hear about Saturday?" asked Renee. Ashley's mom nodded in annoyance because back home Ashley wouldn't shut up about it. Nicole grabbed a bottle of oil and handed it to Renee to assist her in making dinner. She said, "Ashley needs Asia, but doesn't know how to say what's bothering her or fix what she's done. I want to ambush her." In response, Renee said, "That's a wonderful idea because even though Asia has tried, it's not working. The girl just slammed the door and stomped out." As the mothers discussed their daughters' issues, they agreed that both their daughters' emotions and solutions to working this out on their own were not helping them at all. Ashley's mom went to the refrigerator to grab a bottle of water and said, "You know Renee, you were not that great at showing emotions either especially when you felt left out - kind of like Ashley."

Once upon a time, Renee and Nicole were not as close as they are now. One was afraid to invite the other one out because she was worried that the other was no fun, and the other friend was scared to admit that she was lonely, needed friends, and didn't want to keep seeing all the people she worked with on Instagram having a good time without her. All it took was a serious sit-down conversation with Renee and Nicole for them to both admit how they felt. Back when the two moms used to work together at a private school, it was after hours and all the teachers were wrapping up their work to go home. Renee picked up her black school purse, placed her laptop in it, grabbed her water bottle and phone, and left out to go home. On the way out she slowly walked past Nicole's bright orange door with bats pinned on it. She walked slowly because she can hear Nicole making plans with someone about going to a party and all who were going. Renee went to the bathroom which was right next to the front school door. Renee looked at herself in the mirror and said, I know her and I will be great friends, I just have to speak up! Walking out of the bathroom and towards the side of Nicole's classroom door so that she couldn't be seen, Renee took a big inhale, closed her eyes, exhaled and walked into the classroom blurting out, "You know, Nicole, I really don't like how you go out with everyone and don't invite me. I need friends too." Stunned at the statement, Nicole stood up from her desk, grabbed her book bag, water bottle, and purse to leave out and walked up to Renee saying, "Walk with me." In the parking lot both leaning up against the bright green wall on the outside of the building, Nicole said, "Renee, I do think we can be friends but I don't know if you are fun at parties or even want to go. You are so quiet around others and you're always doing things by yourself." Realizing that Nicole had mistaken her quietness and independence for a boring loner, Renee replied, "Well, I've never had people to do things with, but I know I can be fun and have a great time. I really would like to be friends with you and hang out."

That one conversation with these two moms was the beginning of them being honest about how they felt and what they thought. It was also the reason they knew that it was time for their daughters to have a serious conversation as well.

Normally, when these two mothers hung out, it was lots of laughing and music playing in the kitchen, but this time when Asia got up from her bed, she noticed how oddly quiet it was in her home. There was no music playing because the moms wanted to concentrate on how to get the girls together without them being suspicious. Asia slowly walked out of her room and tiptoed down the two steps so that she can spy on the moms. That plan failed because she tripped over a small pumpkin that she forgot to put in the craft room. She heard, "You, okay?" from her mom but said nothing. Then laughing was heard but for a quick moment which was still odd. Asia got up to take the pumpkin to the craft room and walked into the kitchen. The mothers were conversing in a quiet serious manner. Walking into the kitchen, Asia made duck lips and squinted her eyes. Laughing at Asia, Ashley's mom says, "Maybe you and Ash really are sisters. You guys make that same stupid face." Pretending not to hear that, Asia walked to the pantry, grabbed a pack of chocolate chip cookies and walked out of the kitchen but stayed in the living room to eavesdrop on the conversation. She heard lots of things but the only sentence she was confident about was when one of the moms said, "So, tomorrow at 10 a.m." Asia made wide bugs eyes, quickly walked back into her room nervous for whatever lies ahead in her future.

CHAPTER 7

Beep, Beep, Beep. It was 8 am on Saturday and time to get up. Ashley sat up in bed slowly and reached one arm out of the cover to turn the alarm off. She then proceeded to sit up and sluggishly took one leg out of the bed one at a time. Continuing the slow morning process and heading downstairs for breakfast before watching tv, Ashley saw her friend at the dining table. "Good morning, Ash, you are almost there. You've made one change in yourself but there's more and soon you won't see that much of me anymore." While sitting down, talking to her friend Ashley asked, "Why not?" but received no response. Her mom sat down at the dining table and handed Ashley her plate. Beginning to speak, "Are you coming with me to Asia's house tonight?" Ignoring her mother's question while cutting her pancakes into squares, no response was given. "Hello?" With an intense stare at her daughter, Nicole asked again, "Hello?" Looking at her mom and blowing her breath with a pause in-between each word Ashley responded saying, "I… do…. not… feel… comfortable…going." And then took two bites of her pancakes. Since Nicole hadn't begun to eat her breakfast, she sat back in her chair with her arms folded and a straight face waiting on Ashley to communicate better. Nicole had recognized that communicating feelings and being a good person was Ashley's overall issue. Still eating her pancakes, Ashley could feel that her mom was staring and said, "Look, Asia ditched me for

Lauren and basically took my spot in the dance ministry." Well, an hour later after sitting on the couch doing nothing, Ashley's mom said, "Get dressed. Let's go shopping." Excited to take her mind off of how lonely she was feeling, Ashely got dressed and met her mom in the car to leave for the mall. In an effort to distract Ashley from where they were going Ashley's mom took a different route to Asia's house and put on all of her daughter's favorite music like Beyonce, Chris Brown, and Nicki Minaj. When they arrive at Asia's house, her mom said sternly, "Not a word. We are here. Let's go in."

The next series of events are ones that saved Ashley and Asia's relationship with the help of their mothers. Ashley walked up the steps to the living room and didn't see her friend or Asia, but then was told to go sit in the kitchen at the table. Ashley sat low in the chair with almost all of her lower body off of the chair. A few minutes later, Asia walked in and sat at the table. A few more minutes go by Asia was shaking her right leg which she does when she's nervous and Ashley just stared at the clock that was hanging above the refrigerator. Isn't it funny how slow time moves when you want it to and how fast it goes when you don't want it to? A few MORE minutes pass, the moms walked in and Ashley's dance friend walked in. The moms sit in the chairs at the tall counter and the friend sat at the table in between Asia and Ashley. Nicole says, "Enough is enough. Talk it out. The blocking, and not speaking to each other as if you guys aren't best friends and sisters is unacceptable. Fix it."

The silence continued for five more minutes. Renee stepped in, "You will sit here all day until it's fixed. No food, no water, and I will call everyone to cancel the girls' night tonight." Asia sat up in her chair, slammed her hand on the table, and cried, "But Mom!" Renee threw her hand up which was a signal to Asia that meant she didn't want to hear anymore. Asia slugged back down in her chair and took a deep breath. Realizing that she had to speak first because she knew Ashley wouldn't, Asia sat up in her chair and moved her hands to where Ashley could see them while she was talking. She said, "I never wanted to end our friendship until the blocking started and I don't even know why I was blocked." Ashley was still staring at the clock during this statement but moved her head at a quick pace to look at Asia with a smile. It made her happy to know that Asia never wanted to end their friendship. Thinking about how she should respond, Ashley's friend tells her to explain how she felt about Lauren taking everything away from her. Bringing her legs in and using her arms to push herself up to sit upright in the chair, Ashley worked up the courage to come clean and finally say what she had been feeling. She looked at the clock, then at the moms, then down at her hands that were balled up into fists in her lap. She looked at Asia and said, "I felt that you and Lauren were taking everything I loved away from me. From being front and center at dance to you choosing to hang out with her more than me! And when you took the center spot in the anniversary song, I lost it! That's why I blocked you!"

The ice had been broken for these young girls to begin a deeper conversation. Asia immediately responded by saying that she never meant to hurt Ashley when taking center spots, and how it felt good to try something different. Although the most important statement that she made was, "Ashley, we have been close for too long for you not to be honest with your feelings and there is nothing wrong with making new friends." Asia helped Ashley recognize the last change that Ashley needed to make. She helped her realize how fast she was to judge Lauren all because her spot got taken. Looking down at her hands still balled up in fists in between her legs, "You are right." Ashley said and followed up with, "I have to communicate my feelings better and not block you for some stupid jealousy feelings. Also, I can't blame you for what happens at dance." Ashley looked at her mom. Her mom had been saying for the past few weeks that she didn't doesn't need to be in the center all the time to be recognized or validated or to praise God. At the end of the conversation, Ashley acknowledged how much Asia's words meant to her. She discussed how she will work on being a more honest friend and not letting jealousy get to her. She also said how she will work on accepting new people - starting with Lauren. The girls stood up from the table and hug each other for a long time. The moms join in, and finally, someone asked, "Don't we have a girls' night to get ready for?"

The time was12:30 pm and the live episode of Bad Girls Club

would air at 6:00 pm. Ashley and her mom went home to change, and Asia and her mom went to the grocery store to get some more chips, salsa, queso, and of course lemonade for Ashley. Everyone met back at Asia's house and Lauren was the last one to arrive. To embrace the new changes within herself Ashley called out, "Lauren come sit next to me." Looking around first to make sure that Ashley was talking to her, she then looks at Ashley and points at herself with her eyebrows arched. Ashley pointed to herself and nodded her head saying, "Yes, come sit next to me. I know I never really gave you a chance but I think we can be friends." The BGC episode was about to come on but first, a commercial came on about Pitch Perfect a new movie airing and Lauren said, "Yessss, I love that movie!" Ashley loved those movies too and invited Lauren to her house to watch it and get to know each other better and become closer friends. In the end, Ashley had no problem with letting new people into her circle of friends and no problem with where she was placed in dance. All that mattered was how to be a better friend to those around her and having good intentions about why she dances. Watching Ashley interact with Lauren at this girl's night and seeing how far she had come since Lauren was first invited, her dance friend realized that her work was done. Ashley's dance friend hugged Asia and then Ashley saying, "All necessary changes have been made. Be proud." She morphed into Ashley's body as if she was Ashley's inner thoughts and mindset. Looking around seeing that her friend was gone, Ashley looked at Lauren and Asia and smiled. Life was all good in Ashley's world - the perfect group of friends, a great cheer team and church life, and to top it all off there is a cute guy that really likes her. Learning how to be a better friend and taking the steps to become one towards new people has really paid off in Ashley's reality.